Lucy

Zara

Marina

A.J.

Sofia

Hubble

PAPERCUTZ™

MORE GREAT GRAPHIC NOVEL SERIES AVAILABLE FROM PAPERCUTZ™

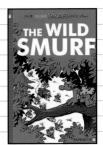
THE SMURFS #21

THE GARFIELD SHOW #6

BARBIE #1

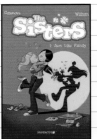
THE SISTERS #1

TROLLS #1

GERONIMO STILTON #17

THEA STILTON #6

SEA CREATURES #1

DINOSAUR EXPLORERS #1

SCARLETT

ANNE OF GREEN BAGELS #1

DRACULA MARRIES FRANKENSTEIN!

THE RED SHOES

THE LITTLE MERMAID

FUZZY BASEBALL

HOTEL TRANSYLVANIA #1

THE LOUD HOUSE #1

MANOSAURS #1

THE ONLY LIVING BOY #5

GUMBY #1

see more at papercutz.com
Also available wherever ebooks are sold.

geeky f@b 5 ™

#3 "DOGgone CATastrophe"

LUCY & LIZ LAREAU — Writers
RYAN JAMPOLE, SUZANNAH ROWNTREE
& SCOTT COUTO — Artists

PAPERCUT Z ™
NEW YORK

geeky f@b 5 ™

#3 "DOGgone CATastrophe"

LUCY & LIZ LAREAU—Writers
SUZANNAH ROWNTREE—Pencil Art, pages 5-28
SCOTT COUTO—Finished Art, pages 5-28
RYAN JAMPOLE—Art, pages 29-54
RYAN JAMPOLE, MATT HERMS—Cover Artists
LAURIE E. SMITH—Colorist, pages 5-19, 21, 23, 24, 26-28
LEONARDO ITO—Colorist, pages 20, 22, 25, 29-54
WILSON RAMOS JR.—Letterer
JEFF WHITMAN—Managing Editor
JIM SALICRUP
Editor-in-Chief

Copyright ©2019 by Geeky Fab Five, Inc. All rights reserved.
All other material © 2019 Papercutz.
papercutz.com
geekyfabfive.com

Hardcover ISBN 978-1-5458-0323-3
Paperback ISBN 978-1-5458-0361-5

Printed in India
September 2019

Papercutz books may be purchased for business or promotional use.
For information on bulk purchases, please contact Macmillan Corporate
and Premium Sales Department at (800) 221-7945 x5442.

Distributed by Macmillan
First Printing

Teacher's Guide available at:
http://papercutz.com/educator-resources-papercutz

CHAPTER ONE: SHELTER IN THE STORM

"WARM SPRING DAYS IN OUR TOWN OF *NORMAL, ILLINOIS*, ARE THE BEST! ESPECIALLY WHEN YOU'RE AT YOUR FRIEND'S *TREEHOUSE* WITH THE *GEEKY FAB 5*. WE CAN FINALLY WEAR SHORTS, HANG OUTSIDE, AND EAT *ZARA'S* CHOCOLATE CHIP COOKIES.

"WELL, EXCEPT FOR *HUBBLE* THE KITTY. HE PREFERS *SQUIRREL SNACKS* OVER CHOCOLATE.

FURRY TREATS WITH TAILS ARE SO *YUMMY!*

ZARA, YOUR TREEHOUSE IS THE *BOMB!*

A.J., YOU SHOULD BUILD CASTLES AFTER COLLEGE!

THANKS, *LUCY!* HEY, *SOFIA*, COME PLAY!

I *AM* PLAYING! SAND AND COMPUTERS ARE SO *NOT* A GOOD COMBO!

♪ "SOMEWHERE OVER THE RAINBOW..." ♪

5

"BUT WOULDN'T YOU KNOW IT? JUST WHEN WE'RE ALL HAVING FUN...

KA-BOOM

WOOSH

WOOSH

KER-RACK

MEOW!

WOOSH

LIGHTNING! WE NEED TO GET AWAY FROM THE TREEHOUSE. NOW!

WOOSH

I NEED SPACE

6

WREEE-EEE-EEE

GIRLS, HURRY! AWAY FROM THE TREES! TO THE BASEMENT, NOW!

WREEE-EEE-EEE

ZARA, WHAT IS THAT SOUND?

STORM SIRENS!

WHOA, SOFIA, CHECK OUT THOSE COOL CLOUDS!

A.J., YOU ARE SOOO WEIRD! TORNADOS ARE SCARY AND DANGEROUS!

WHAT'S SCARY AND DANGEROUS IS MY PURRFECT FUR GETTING WET!

I'M MELTING...!

7

"WE MADE IT TO ZARA'S BASEMENT JUST IN TIME. **MR. KUMAR** CALLED OUR PARENTS SO THEY KNEW WE WERE SAFE INSIDE...

STORM REPORT

LIVE FROM WYXZ, WE ARE UNDER A **TORNADO WARNING** UNTIL 5 P.M. A TORNADO TOUCHED DOWN NORTHWEST OF THE NORMAL CITY LIMITS. TAKE SHELTER NOW.

GO TO A BASEMENT OR ROOM WITH NO WINDOWS OR FIND A CLOSET ON THE LOWEST FLOOR.

LISTEN TO THAT **WIND** OUTSIDE! IT SOUNDS LIKE A **FREIGHT TRAIN!**

TORNADOS MAKE THAT SOUND, **MARINA**...WHEN THE WIND IS BLOWING LIKE **OVER 100** MILES PER HOUR!

THAT'S A **FAST** WIND! WE DIDN'T GET MANY TORNADO WARNINGS AT OUR OLD HOUSE IN VIRGINIA.

WELL, WE LIVE IN **TORNADO ALLEY**, SO WE GET A LOT.

TORNADO ALLEY?

YEAH, ILLINOIS AND OTHER STATES IN THE MIDDLE ARE RIGHT IN TORNADO ALLEY. THEY HAPPEN WHEN WARM, STEAMY AIR FROM THE GULF OF MEXICO, SMACKS INTO THE COLD AIR FROM CANADA...PRESTO! YOU GET A TORNADO!

SPEAKING OF **WARM AIR** FROM THE SOUTH...

≥FART≤

PEE-EWWW! STINKY KITTY!

8

"AS THE THUNDER BOOMS AND LIGHTNING FLASHES, A FAMILIAR FRIEND OF THE GEEKY FAB 5 APPEARS ON TV...

THIS IS SUZY PUNDERGAST, REPORTING LIVE FROM NORMAL. TREES AND POWER LINES ARE DOWN. WINDS ARE DAMAGING, BUT THE STORM SHOULD PASS IN THE NEXT FEW MINUTES.

MY SUZY... SO BRAVE! STAY SAFE, MY LOVE!

IT'S SUZY!

THE NATIONAL WEATHER SERVICE REPORTS A TORNADO HAS RIPPED THROUGH THE NORTH SIDE OF THE CITY. MANY HOMES ARE DAMAGED.

THIS IS TERRIBLE. I HOPE NO ONE HAS BEEN HURT.

IT SOUNDS LIKE THE WIND HAS DIED DOWN. LISTEN! NO SIRENS!

LET'S GO SEE WHAT HAPPENED.

I NEED SPACE

9

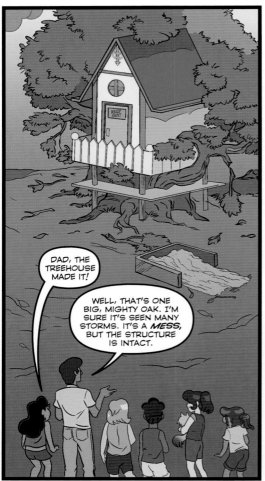

DAD, THE TREEHOUSE MADE IT!

WELL, THAT'S ONE BIG, MIGHTY OAK. I'M SURE IT'S SEEN MANY STORMS. IT'S A *MESS*, BUT THE STRUCTURE IS INTACT.

MEOW! MEOW!

HUBBLE, WHAT IS IT, BOY?

I NEED

MY *HUBBLE-SENSE* IN TINGLING! THIS LOOKS LIKE A JOB FOR *SUPER-HUBBLE!*

HUBBLE IS *RUNNING AWAY!* I HOPE IT'S NOT BECAUSE I CALLED HIM "STINKY KITTY."

HE'S *NOT* RUNNING AWAY, SOFIA. HE'S RUNNING *TO* THE TREEHOUSE...!

I THINK HUBBLE HAS FOUND SOMETHING *UNDER* THE TREEHOUSE...

MEOW! MEOW! MEOW!

SEE ANYTHING, MARINA?

IT'S DARK UNDER HERE, LUCY. LET ME REACH IN...OH! I FEEL *FURRY* THINGS!

CAN IT BE WHAT I THINK IT IS?

IT IS!

WHAT?! WHAT DID YOU FIND?!

LOOK WHAT HUBBLE FOUND! *KITTIES!*

THERE'S ONE MORE!

UNDER A WET TREEHOUSE IS NO PLACE FOR KITTIES.

11

THEY MUST HAVE SHELTERED UNDER THE TREEHOUSE DURING THE STORM.

CLICK

WHERE IS THE *MAMA* KITTY? I HOPE SHE IS OKAY...

FINDING THE KITTIES' MOM COULD BE A NEW MISSION FOR *GEEKY FAB 5.*

OH, THEY ARE SO *CUTE!* DAD--?

DON'T EVEN *THINK* ABOUT IT, ZARA! YOU KNOW YOUR MOM IS *ALLERGIC* TO CATS. THESE KITTIES NEED TO GO TO THE ANIMAL SHELTER WHERE A VETERINARIAN WILL EXAMINE THEM.

GOOD JOB, HUBBLE!

CAN WE GO WITH YOU, MR. KUMAR? WE CAN PET THE OTHER SHELTER CATS.

RRRRRRR

WHY NOT KEEP PETTING ME?! MORE KITTY MASSAGE, PLEEEASE...

12

CHAPTER TWO: DOGgone CATastrophe

"MR. KUMAR CALLED OUR PARENTS TO TELL THEM WE WERE OKAY. OUR NEIGHBORHOOD WAS FINE, BUT ON THE WAY TO THE SHELTER, WE SAW STORM DAMAGE EVERYWHERE..."

OH, DAD. LOOK! THIS NEIGHBORHOOD GOT HIT WAY WORSE THAN OURS.

TORNADOS CAN DAMAGE ONE PART OF TOWN AND LEAVE ANOTHER PART ALONE. THEIR PATHS ARE HARD TO PREDICT.

"WE ARE ALL THINKING THE SAME THING: 'HOW COULD THIS HAPPEN?'"

"WHEN WE ARRIVE AT THE SHELTER, WE CAN'T BELIEVE OUR EYES..."

MCCLEAN COUNTY NO-KILL ANIMAL SHELTER

"A.J., OUR ENGINEER-IN-TRAINING, CAN'T STAND TO SEE SUCH DAMAGE..

THE ANIMALS BETTER BE OKAY...

13

HELLO! I'M *DR. KATRINA CHO*, BUT EVERYONE CALLS ME, *"KAT."* SORRY YOU HAD TO WAIT. WE'VE BEEN CLEANING UP. WE'RE SCRAMBLING TO MAKE THE ANIMALS COMFORTABLE. THE TREE CAVED IN THE ROOF, SO THE RAIN CAME IN. EVERYTHING IS SOAKED.

SPAY

YOUR NAME IS KAT? AS IN *KITTY CATS?*

YES! I LOVE KITTIES! I ONLY HAVE A FEW MINUTES. *WYXZ* IS COMING TO REPORT A NEWS STORY ON OUR DAMAGE. HOW MAY I HELP YOU?

WELL, THIS PROBABLY ISN'T THE BEST TIME, BUT...WE FOUND ORPHANED KITTENS THAT NEED A VET AND A KENNEL UNTIL THEY CAN BE ADOPTED.

MEW.

OH, MY. LET ME TAKE A QUICK CHECK FOR *BROKEN BONES.* THEY LOOK LIKE THEY STILL NEED THEIR MOTHER. WE HAVE FORMULA TO FEED THEM, BUT I'M AFRAID THIS IS NO FANCY *KITTY HOTEL.*

OUR CAT ROOM IS FLOODED ALONG WITH THE DOG KENNELS. WE HAVE TO KEEP THE ANIMALS IN THEIR CAGES FOR NOW.

DING-DONG

MEW.

MEW.

MEW.

14

HI, SUZY!

WELL, HELLO! IT'S MY FAVORITE GO-GETTER GIRLS, THE GEEKY FAB 5! WHAT BRINGS YOU HERE AFTER THIS CRAZY STORM?

WE SAW YOU ON *TV!* I LOVE YOUR RED RAIN BOOTS, SUZY!

SOFIA, *FOCUS.* WE FOUND THREE ORPHANED KITTIES AFTER THE STORM.

WE BROUGHT THEM HERE, BUT THE SHELTER IS *WRECKED!*

THESE ANIMALS NEED OUR HELP!

I COULD HELP *FIX IT!*

OH, MY. YOU ALL KNOW EACH OTHER?

YES, DR. CHO. AND LET ME SAY THAT THESE GIRLS AND MS. PUNDERGAST ARE *UNSTOPPABLE* WHEN PEOPLE AND ANIMALS NEED HELP.

WHY NOT GIVE US ALL A TOUR? YOU CAN TRUST THEM!

15

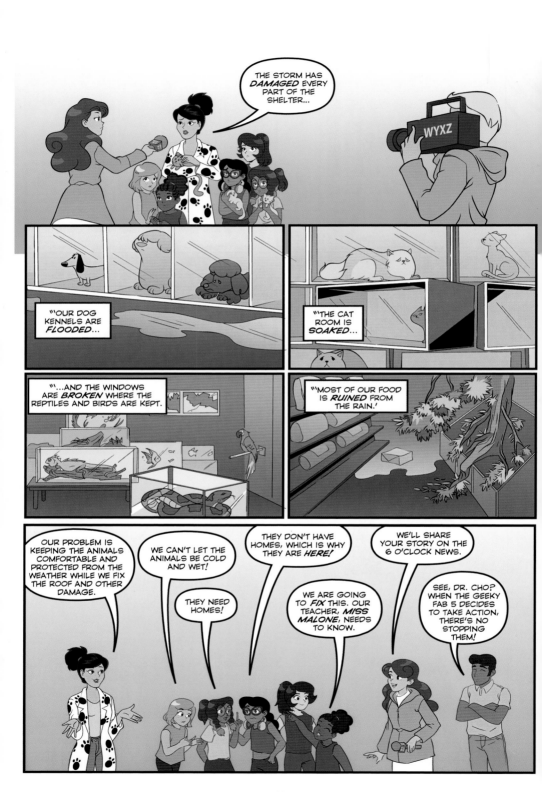

THE STORM HAS *DAMAGED* EVERY PART OF THE SHELTER...

WYXZ

"'OUR DOG KENNELS ARE *FLOODED*...

"'THE CAT ROOM IS *SOAKED*...

"'...AND THE WINDOWS ARE *BROKEN* WHERE THE REPTILES AND BIRDS ARE KEPT.

"'MOST OF OUR FOOD IS *RUINED* FROM THE RAIN.'

OUR PROBLEM IS KEEPING THE ANIMALS COMFORTABLE AND PROTECTED FROM THE WEATHER WHILE WE FIX THE ROOF AND OTHER DAMAGE.

WE CAN'T LET THE ANIMALS BE COLD AND WET!

THEY DON'T HAVE HOMES, WHICH IS WHY THEY ARE *HERE!*

WE'LL SHARE YOUR STORY ON THE 6 O'CLOCK NEWS.

THEY NEED HOMES!

WE ARE GOING TO *FIX* THIS. OUR TEACHER, *MISS MALONE*, NEEDS TO KNOW.

SEE, DR. CHO? WHEN THE GEEKY FAB 5 DECIDES TO TAKE ACTION, THERE'S NO STOPPING THEM!

16

CHAPTER THREE: CODERS TO THE RESCUE

"IT'S MONDAY. MISS MALONE IS OUR FOURTH GRADE TEACHER AT EARHART ELEMENTARY. SHE'S SUPER COOL AND BELIEVES THAT WE SHOULD BE COURAGEOUS LIKE OUR SCHOOL'S NAMESAKE AND FAMOUS PILOT, AMELIA EARHART.

GOOD MORNING. I SEE YOU ALL SURVIVED THE STORM. ARE YOUR FAMILIES AND HOMES OKAY?

THE TORNADO MISSED OUR NEIGHBORHOOD, BUT THE COUNTY ANIMAL SHELTER IS DESTROYED! WE NEED TO FIX IT!

A TREE CRASHED THROUGH THE ROOF AND IT IS FLOODED PRETTY BADLY.

DR. CHO SAYS THEY CAN'T FIX THE SHELTER WHILE THE ANIMALS ARE THERE.

YEAH, AND ALL THEIR FOOD AND TOYS ARE GARBAGE BECAUSE OF THE RAIN.

YES, I SAW SUZY'S REPORT ON LAST NIGHT'S TV NEWS. I SUPPOSE YOU ALL HAVE AN IDEA ON HOW TO BE A FORCE FOR GOOD? HMMM?

NOT YET. BUT WE'LL THINK OF SOMETHING!

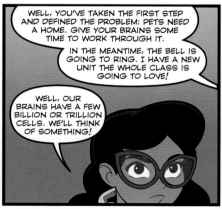

WELL, YOU'VE TAKEN THE FIRST STEP AND DEFINED THE PROBLEM: PETS NEED A HOME. GIVE YOUR BRAINS SOME TIME TO WORK THROUGH IT.

IN THE MEANTIME, THE BELL IS GOING TO RING. I HAVE A NEW UNIT THE WHOLE CLASS IS GOING TO LOVE!

WELL, OUR BRAINS HAVE A FEW BILLION OR TRILLION CELLS. WE'LL THINK OF SOMETHING!

RRRRINNNGGG

17

GOOD MORNING, EARHART STUDENTS! AS YOUR PRINCIPAL, I WANT TO WELCOME YOU BACK. I'M GLAD YOU ARE HERE SAFE AND SOUND. WE KNOW, HOWEVER, THAT HOMES AND BUSINESSES WERE DAMAGED...

WE HAVE PLACED BINS AT EACH DOOR SO PLEASE ASK YOUR FAMILIES TO HELP DONATE TO OUR FELLOW STUDENTS' FAMILIES WHO MAY NEED ITEMS SUCH AS RAGS, CLEANER, BLEACH, MOPS OR BROOMS. THANK YOU!

THANK YOU, *MRS. HOLIDAY*. GOOD MORNING, CLASS. IS EVERYONE HERE *OKAY?*

YEAH, BUT WE LOST POWER SO MY BROTHER WENT CRAZY WHEN HE COULDN'T PLAY GAMES ON THE INTERNET!

YES, WE LOVE OUR PHONES AND COMPUTERS, DON'T WE? SPEAKING OF COMPUTERS, WE'RE STARTING A NEW UNIT TODAY. WHO CAN TELL ME WHAT *"APPS"* ARE? SOFIA...?

THEY ARE PROGRAMS WE USE TO DO CERTAIN THINGS ON OUR PHONES OR COMPUTERS, LIKE EMAIL, SURF THE INTERNET, OR OTHER THINGS.

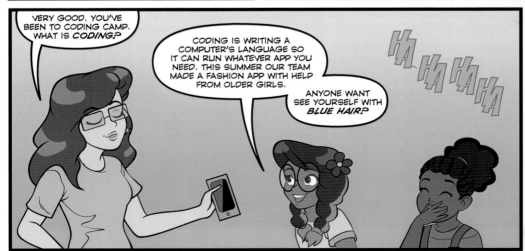

VERY GOOD. YOU'VE BEEN TO CODING CAMP. WHAT IS *CODING?*

CODING IS WRITING A COMPUTER'S LANGUAGE SO IT CAN RUN WHATEVER APP YOU NEED. THIS SUMMER OUR TEAM MADE A FASHION APP WITH HELP FROM OLDER GIRLS.

ANYONE WANT SEE YOURSELF WITH *BLUE HAIR?*

HA HA HA HA HA

TODAY *YOU* WILL ALL START LEARNING WHY AND HOW TO CREATE A COMPUTER APP WITH THE HELP OF A VERY *SPECIAL FRIEND.*

AWESOME!

COOL.

CAN I MAKE A BILLION DOLLARS LIKE THOSE PROGRAMMERS?

HA! LET'S ASK *MR. TACKETT.* HE IS OUR COMPUTER LAB TEACHER AT EARHART. HE WILL BE HELPING US FOR THE NEXT TWO WEEKS IN COMPUTER LAB. EVERYONE SAY, "HI!"

HI, MR. TACKETT!

HI, EVERYONE! WHAT DO YOU LIKE TO DO ON YOUR COMPUTERS?

PLAY GAMES!

MY GRANDPA FINDS DATES!

BUY STUFF!

THE COOL THING IS THAT PROGRAMMERS LOVE TO FIND NEW WAYS TO USE COMPUTERS. IT'S LIKE SOLVING PUZZLES EVERY DAY!

THINK ABOUT IT. YOUR MOM WANTS TO KNOW IF YOU NEED AN UMBRELLA. THAT'S A PROBLEM WEATHER APPS CAN SOLVE.

WANT A NEW PAIR OF SHOES? SHOP ONLINE.

YOUR GRANDPA IS LONELY. HE USES AN APP TO FIND NEW FRIENDS.

WHAT PUZZLES? I HATE *CROSSWORDS!*

19

WHAT PROBLEM SHALL WE SOLVE TOGETHER TODAY?

DIDN'T SOME OF YOU COME TO ME WITH A PROBLEM CAUSED BY THE TORNADO?

MAKE MY SISTER SHUT UP!

DO MY HOMEWORK FOR ME!

HA HA HA HA HA

YEAH! WE NEED TO HELP THE ANIMAL SHELTER.

OH, NO! ARE THE ANIMALS OKAY?

YES. DURING THE STORM, THE KENNELS WERE FLOODED BECAUSE A TREE FELL ON THE BUILDING. THEY NEED A NEW ROOF, BUT HAVE TO MOVE THE ANIMALS FIRST.

SO, THE ANIMALS NEED HOMES?

WHAT IF THE ANIMALS ARE LONELY LIKE MY GRANDPA? HE FINDS NICE FRIENDS ON HIS PHONE APP. CAN WE MAKE AN APP FOR THE ANIMALS?

THAT'S A GREAT IDEA! CLASS, READY TO SOLVE A PUZZLE?

YEAH!

SO AWESOME!

20

"IT IS OUR FIRST DAY OF COMPUTER LAB. WE ARE SO EXCITED TO HELP THE SHELTER PETS FIND HOMES. MR. TACKETT IS READY TO SHOW US HOW WE CAN BUILD AN APP TO CONNECT PETS WITH PEOPLE...

LET'S GET STARTED. THE ANIMAL SHELTER GAVE ME PICTURES OF ALL PETS THAT NEED TO BE FOSTERED DURING CONSTRUCTION.

NOW, FOR PEOPLE TO BE MATCHED WITH THE *RIGHT* PET, WE MUST ORGANIZE THE ANIMALS IN WAYS SOMEONE MIGHT CHOOSE THEM.

LIKE DOGS, CATS, OR SNAKES?

RIGHT!

"NOW, LET'S GROUP EACH PET BY TRAITS SUCH AS: SIZE, FUR FLUFFINESS, OR WEIGHT. SOME MIGHT WANT A BIG DOG, OTHERS, SMALLER DOGS LIKE PUGS."

WE HAVE *MORE* THAN JUST DOGS AND CATS. HOW WOULD YOU ORGANIZE THE SNAKE, THE GUINEA PIGS, OR THE MACAW?

MAYBE GROUP THEM AS REPTILES FOR LIZARDS AND SNAKES; BIRDS ARE THEIR OWN GROUP; AND THE GUINEA PIGS COULD BE--

RODENTS!

MY MOM *HATES* MICE. EW!

21

WHAT ELSE WOULD ANY *POTENTIAL PET-OWNER* WANT TO THINK ABOUT WHEN CHOOSING A PET?

HOW ABOUT... IF THE PET KNOWS HOW TO GO POOP OUTSIDE!

ALLERGIES! MY MOM IS ALLERGIC TO CATS!

HA HA HA HA HA A.J. SAID *"POOP"!*

HA HA HA HA

ALLERGIES ARE A CONCERN. AND YES, MANY PEOPLE WANT A PET ALREADY *HOUSEBROKEN* OR *POTTY-TRAINED!* ANY OTHER TRAITS A PET-OWNER THINKS ABOUT?

WHAT KIND OF *FOOD* THEY NEED? SNAKES EAT MICE!

GREAT JOB! TO FIND THE PERFECT PET, THEY NEED LOTS OF *INFORMATION.*

SPECIAL *TOYS?*

DO THE PETS *BITE?*

NOW, I AM GOING TO ORGANIZE ALL OF THESE PETS BY COLOR, WEIGHT, EXERCISE, AND THE OTHER TRAITS WE TALKED ABOUT, IN A LANGUAGE THE COMPUTER WILL UNDERSTAND.

NEXT WEEK WE'LL WORK ON OUR NEW APP.

"SOFIA STAYS AFTER CLASS...

MR. TACKETT, ARE YOU GOING TO MAKE A *DATABASE* TO ORGANIZE THE ANIMALS?

YOU KNOW WHAT A DATABASE IS?

YEP. I WENT TO A CODING CAMP. IT'S A WAY TO ORGANIZE THE INFORMATION SO THE COMPUTER CAN FIND IT. MAY I HELP YOU AFTER SCHOOL?

OF COURSE! LET'S GET TO WORK.

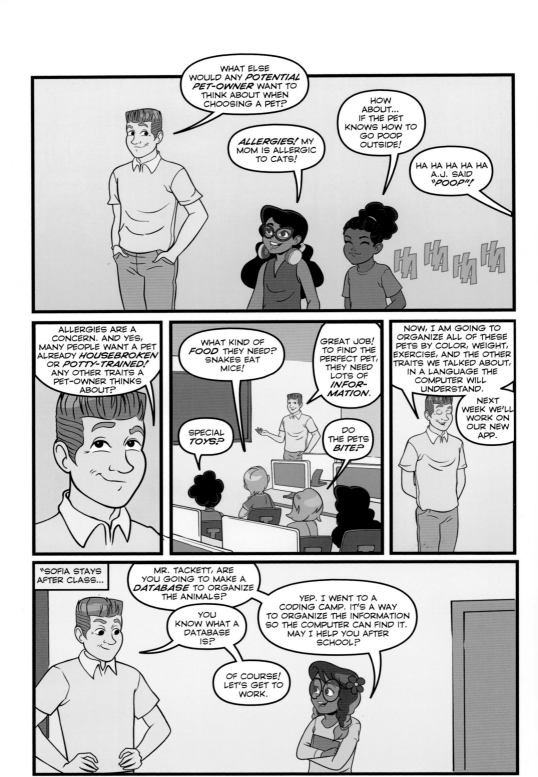

22

"SOFIA AND MR. TACKETT WORK TO ORGANIZE ALL THE WAYS AN OWNER COULD CHOOSE A PET.

OKAY, I'VE GOT ALL OF THE PET INFO INTO DIFFERENT CATEGORIES, SO OWNERS CAN PICK THE RIGHT PET.

COOL! NOW LET'S THINK ABOUT HOW SOMEONE WOULD SEE THE CHOICES AND THEN TRY IT!

"SOFIA TESTS THE APP TO SEE IF IT SHE WILL GET THE RIGHT PET. SHE PICKS HER FAVORITE PET TRAITS FOR A DOG.

CHOOSE YOUR PET:
CAT
DOG
RODENT
SNAKE
BIRD

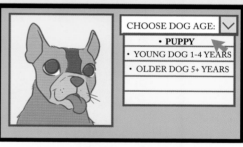

CHOOSE DOG AGE:
• **PUPPY**
• YOUNG DOG 1-4 YEARS
• OLDER DOG 5+ YEARS

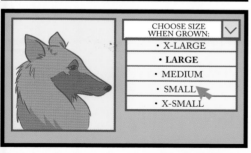

CHOOSE SIZE WHEN GROWN:
• X-LARGE
• **LARGE**
• MEDIUM
• SMALL
• X-SMALL

CHOOSE FUR COLOR AND LENGTH
• BLACK   **FLUFFY**
• **WHITE** SHORT HAIR
• BROWN LONG HAIR
• OTHER

WANT MY DOG TO:
• HUNT
• TAKE WALKS
• PLAY NICE WITH KIDS
• SLEEP IN A KENNEL
• **SIT ON MY LAP**

YOUR PERFECT PET!
NAME: **LARRY**

23

UH, MR. TACKETT. I CHOSE A WHITE, FLUFFY PUPPY DOG THAT SITS ON MY LAP. *NOT* LARRY THE GREEN LIZARD!

OH, BOY. THAT'S WHAT CODERS CALL A *"BUG!"*

NO, THAT'S A *CHINESE DRAGON LIZARD.* IT *EATS* BUGS!

HAHA!

YOU KNOW THAT BUGS ARE *MISTAKES* IN THE CODE, REMEMBER? WHEN YOU MAKE A MISTAKE, TRY AGAIN. THAT'S THE FUN PART! LET'S MAKE SURE LARRY GETS THE RIGHT HOME!

24

"IT TOOK A LOT OF HARD WORK, BUT SOFIA AND MR. TACKETT ARE READY FOR THE CLASS TO TEST THE NEW APP...

SOFIA AND I ARE EXCITED TO SHOW YOU THE APP, BUT IT IS *NOT* FINISHED! WE NEED YOU TO TEST IT AND SEE IF WE WORKED OUT ALL THE BUGS!

COOL! I GOT THE PYTHON NAMED *PETE!*

OOOH, THESE HAMSTERS HAVE BIG WHISKERS! IT'S SO FUN TO PICK YOUR PETS!

"*PICK YOUR PETS*"? HEY, THAT'S A COOL NAME, *CINDY!*

PICKURPETZ!

CINDY, THAT'S A GREAT APP NAME!

WOO-HOO!

25

"THE SHELTER ANIMALS ARE DEPENDING ON US. AND THANKS TO MR. TACKETT AND SOFIA, OUR CLASS HELPED CREATE OUR PICKURPETZ APP.

WELL DONE, CLASS! PICKURPETZ IS WORKING PERFECTLY! OUR PRINCIPAL, MRS. HOLIDAY, HAS SOME FRIENDS FOR YOU TO MEET!

I AM SO PROUD OF ALL OF YOU. OUR STUDENTS SOAR, JUST LIKE AMELIA EARHART! LET'S WELCOME OUR SPECIAL GUESTS!

HEY, SUZY! HI, DR. CHO!

YES, MEET DR. CHO, THE DIRECTOR AND VETERINARIAN AT THE McCLEAN COUNTY NO-KILL ANIMAL SHELTER. WE ALSO INVITED SUZY PUNDERGAST FROM WYXZ-TV...SHE IS HERE TO LEARN ABOUT YOUR NEW APP.

ON BEHALF OF OUR ANIMALS, *THANK YOU!*

IF WE CAN FOSTER THESE PETS TO CARING PEOPLE, WE CAN FINISH OUR REPAIRS AND MAKE THEIR HOME NEW AGAIN!

DR. CHO, WHAT ELSE CAN WE DO TO *HELP* THE ANIMALS?

YEAH, SO COOL!

I'VE GOT AN IDEA! WHAT IF WE PUT ON A *PET PARADE* AT OUR SCHOOL? INSTEAD OF TICKETS, PEOPLE COULD DONATE PET FOOD AND TOYS.

I BET I CAN TEACH A *DOG* A COOL TRICK!

I'LL TAKE A *KITTY!*

LOOKS LIKE ANOTHER EARHART STORY THAT'S GOING TO MAKE A DIFFERENCE. BUT RIGHT NOW WE'RE HERE TO TALK ABOUT YOU NEW APP! ROLL CAMERAS!

WYXZ

CHAPTER FOUR: PICKURPETZ IN ACTION!

PickURPetz

HANK

"OUR *PICKURPETZ* APP IS WORKING! OUR TOWN OF NORMAL IS STEPPING UP TO TAKE CARE OF THE ANIMALS UNTIL THE ROOF GETS FIXED!

BRUTUS & BUTCH
MATCHED!

ROGER & RONNIE
MATCHED!

SPHINX AND SYBIL
MATCHED!

RUFFLES AND RUSSELL
MATCHED!

GOLDIE AND GORDON
MATCHED!

LARRY & LOUIS
MATCHED!

WELL, GIRLS, WE ARE DOWN TO OUR LAST ORPHANS. ALL THE OTHER PETS HAVE HOMES.

NO ONE WANTS THEM? HMMM... I COULD TAKE THIS *BIRD.* I WONDER IF SHE CAN SING?

THAT *STANDARD POODLE* IS SOOOO CLASSY. HE'S MINE.

I'LL TAKE THE *BASSETT HOUND* WITH THE BROKEN LEGS. I WONDER IF I COULD MAKE HIM A WHEELCHAIR?

THOSE LITTLE *GUINEA PIGS* ARE SO ADORABLE AND SMART. HI, SWEETIES!

I GUESS THAT LEAVES THE *CORN SNAKE.* WE'LL TAKE HER.

EEEK! NO SNAKES IN OUR HOUSE, LUCY!

HAVE THEY GONE *CUCKOO?* WHY HAVE ANOTHER PET, WHEN YOU ALREADY HAVE *ME?*

28

HANK & SUZY
MATCHED!

JOSIE & ZARA
MATCHED!

ADA & GRACE & SOFIA
MATCHED!

BO & A.J.
MATCHED!

CALLA & LUCY & MARINA
MATCHED!

CHAPTER FIVE: PETS ARE PEOPLE TOO!

"A NEW PET NEEDS TIME TO FEEL COZY, AND OWNERS HAVE TO ADJUST TOO. SOME ARE TEACHING THEIR ANIMALS TRICKS FOR THE UPCOMING PET PARADE. BUT OTHERS, LIKE MARINA, HAVE TO GET OVER THEIR FEAR...

I NAMED HER "CALLA," THE CORN SNAKE. SHE'S TAME AND SUPER FRIENDLY. SHE'S *NOT* GONNA BITE!

GET THAT *SSSSS-NNNAAKE* OUT OF HERE *NOW!* I *HATE* SNAKES!

YEAH! *SLITHER OFF,* SNAKE!

IT'S OKAY, CALLA. DON'T WORRY ABOUT MARINA. SHE FREAKS OUT AT EVERYTHING.

I'M GOING TO GO PLAY. SEE YA!

"WHILE I GO AWAY, HUBBLE WANTS TO PLAY!

LOOK, PAL. YOU MAY BE A NICE SNAKE, BUT *THIS IS MY HOUSE,* OKAY?

IT'S TIME I BREAK YOU OUT OF JAIL, AND SET YOU FREE.

SWAT

THANK'SSSSSSSS.

BUH-BYE.

MEANWHILE AT A.J.'S HOUSE, *BO THE BASSET HOUND* IS IN GOOD HANDS. A.J. LIKES ROBOTICS. HER DAD IS AN ENGINEER WHO BUILDS BRIDGES. HER BROTHER, *SAM*, IS GOING TO COLLEGE AND WANTS TO STUDY ENGINEERING TOO.

I THINK YOUR IDEA FOR A *WHEELCHAIR* IS A GOOD ONE, A.J.

BUT HOW DO WE DESIGN ONE FOR A DOG?

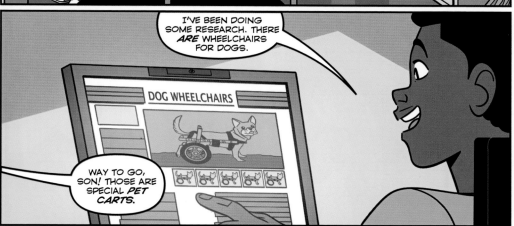

I'VE BEEN DOING SOME RESEARCH. THERE *ARE* WHEELCHAIRS FOR DOGS.

DOG WHEELCHAIRS

WAY TO GO, SON! THOSE ARE SPECIAL *PET CARTS*.

BO, WE'LL GET YOU MOVING, BUDDY.

SLOW DOWN, A.J., WE ARE NOT EVEN SURE IF BO CAN BE FITTED FOR ONE. WE NEED TO TALK TO DR. CHO FIRST.

31

"IT'S SATURDAY MORNING, AND A.J. IS SO EXCITED FOR BO AND ALSO TO SEE THE SHELTER UNDER CONSTRUCTION...

LOOK! THEY'RE BUILDING THE NEW ROOF!

BANG BANG BANG

MCCLEAN COUNTY NO-KILL ANIMAL SHELTER

HEY, DR. CHO. THIS IS MY DAD AND MY BROTHER, SAM. YOU ALREADY KNOW BO!

NICE TO MEET YOU! HOW IS BO?

WE CAME TO TALK TO YOU ABOUT GETTING BO A WHEELCHAIR.

WHAT A GREAT IDEA! HIS LEGS WERE BROKEN IN THE STORM BUT I STILL HOPE HE WILL MAKE A RECOVERY. WE CAN FIT HIM FOR A CHAIR, BUT THEY COST OVER $100.

THAT IS TOO EXPENSIVE FOR THE SHELTER. I'M SORRY, A.J.

PLEASE, DAD? YOU CAN HAVE MY COIN JAR...I CAN DO CHORES... AND--

I CAN HELP, TOO.

IN THAT CASE, I HAVE A LIST OF CHORES AT HOME FOR YOU TWO TO EARN BO'S WHEELS. I AM PROUD OF YOU BOTH FOR CARING MORE ABOUT BO THAN STUFF YOU COULD BUY.

BO, WE'LL GET YOU ROLLING IN NO TIME!

32

FIRST, LET'S *WEIGH* HIM ON THE TABLE. THEN, A.J., I'LL NEED YOUR HELP TO MEASURE BO FOR HIS CART. HOLD HIM...

52 POUNDS. PERFECT WEIGHT! NOW, TIME TO MEASURE HIM. A.J., COME TAKE A LOOK AT THIS POSTER OF A DOG'S *SKELETON!*

WE NEED TO MEASURE HIS LENGTH. HERE IS HIS ARMPIT, CALLED THE *AXILLA*. WE NEED TO MEASURE FROM HERE ALL THE WAY TO THE TAIL.

FOR HEIGHT, MEASURE FROM THE FLOOR TO HIS *FLANK*. THE FLANK IS WHERE THE HIND LEG MEETS HIS STOMACH. READY?

GOT IT!

OKAY, FIRST THE *LENGTH.*

28 INCHES.

GOOD JOB MEASURING HIS FLANK. LASTLY, HOW TALL IS HIS FRONT?

COOL. IT'S 12 INCHES.

IT'S GOING TO BE AT LEAST A WEEK OR TWO FOR THE CART TO BE DELIVERED. THEN, WE'LL FIT HIM AND TEACH HIM HOW TO WALK WITH IT. BE SURE TO BRING *DOGGIE TREATS* FOR TRAINING!

THANKS SO MUCH, DR. CHO.

HOOOOOWLLLLL

33

"WHILE BO IS GETTING FITTED FOR HIS CART, SUZY IS GIVING HANK THE *MOVIE STAR TREATMENT* AT HIS VERY OWN SPA DAY...

I ABSOLUTELY ADORE THIS POODLE!

WHY WAS HE IN THE SHELTER? HE LOOKS LIKE A PURE-BRED.

HIS NAME IS *HANK.* DR. CHO SAID HE WAS A SHOW POODLE THAT NEVER WON A BLUE RIBBON, SO HIS OWNERS ABANDONED HIM. HE'S GORGEOUS AND SO SMART!

"MANI-PEDI'S ARE ALSO A *MUST!*

YOU ARE GOING TO LOOK *MAR-VE-LOUS* FOR EARHART'S PET PARADE, SWEETIE!

⸗MWAH!⸞

WOOF!

34

"IT'S NOT JUST OUR FOUR-LEGGED FOSTER PETS GETTING ALL THE ATTENTION...ZARA AND JOSIE ARE GROOVING AT PRACTICE FOR THE *EARHART PET PARADE*...

I KNOW MACAWS ARE SMART ENOUGH TO *TALK*... SO...?

NEVER MIND.

WHAAA?!

NEVER MIND.

JOSIE! YOU WON'T ROCK THE PARADE IF YOU DON'T SHOW SOME MORE *TALENT!*

YOU NEED TO TALK *AND* SING, I'LL PLAY THIS RECORDING OVER AND OVER, SO YOU CAN REPEAT WHAT YOU HEAR, OKAY? LET'S DO A LITTLE *MELBOURNE SHUFFLE!*

NEVER MIND.

♫ *"PARTY ROCK IN THE HOUSE TONIGHT..."* ♫

♫ *"EVERYDAY I'M SHUFFLING..."* ♫

PARTY ROCK!

35

"SOFIA'S GUINEA PIGS AREN'T LEFT OUT EITHER! SOFIA IS A *FASHIONISTA* AND *CRAFTY ARTIST* WHO LOVES TO MAKE GLITTERY COSTUMES, EVEN FOR FURRY FRIENDS.

I CAN'T BELIEVE YOU TWO HAVE THE SAME NAMES AS MY TWO COMPUTER HEROES, *ADA LOVELACE* AND *GRACE HOPPER.*

LET'S *BLING* YOU UP!

OKAY, ADA AND GRACE, LET'S SEE YOU SHINE! AS GUINEA PIG *COSPLAYERS!*

FLASH

PRINCESS *LEIA* AND *REY!*

FLASH

FLASH

36

CHAPTER SIX: SNAKES AND DOGS ON THE RUN

"HELPING OUR SHELTER PETS MAKES US HUNGRY. GOOD THING MOM MADE MY FAVORITE DINNER... SPAGHETTI!

MARINA, HONEY, WHERE *IS* YOUR SISTER?

SHE WAS MAKING A LOT OF *NOISE*...IT SOUNDED LIKE SHE WAS *DESTROYING* HER ROOM OR SOMETHING.

LUCCCCY! DINNER!

"BUT BEFORE I COULD EVEN THINK ABOUT EATING...

DANG IT, CALLA, *WHERE* ARE YOU? MOM AND MARINA WILL SO *FREAK!*

LUCILLE KAY MONROE!

IF YOU ARE NOT DOWNSTAIRS IN 3...2...

COMING!

GRACIOUS SAKES ALIVE! WHAT WERE YOU DOING?

UH...GRACIOUS *SNAKES?* ER... *SAKES!* NOTHING, MOM...NOTHING.

SO, THE FUN BEGINS...

SLUUUURP

37

SO, GIRLS, HOW GOES THE ANIMAL SHELTER PROJECT?

REALLY COOL! ALL THE PETS ARE MATCHED WITH FOSTER OWNERS. NOW VOLUNTEERS CAN BEGIN TO FIX THE ROOF AND CLEAN UP THE INSIDE. DR. CHO IS AMAZING!

LUCY, HOW IS CALLA? I HAD SECOND THOUGHTS ABOUT LETTING HER STAY, BUT CORN SNAKES ARE SUPPOSED TO BE VERY SWEET AND TAME.

AND, I MUST ADMIT, YOU HAVE TAKEN VERY GOOD CARE OF HER!

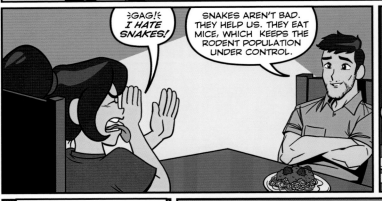

⸮GAG!⸮ I HATE SNAKES!

SNAKES AREN'T BAD. THEY HELP US. THEY EAT MICE, WHICH KEEPS THE RODENT POPULATION UNDER CONTROL.

EATING RODENTS IS MY JOB. NO SNAKES ALLOWED.

UHHH...MOM...DAD... MARINA... I NEED TO TELL YOU SOMETHING....

YES...?

38

CALLA HAS...UH... *SLITHERED OFF...*

WHAT?!

SHE'S GONE?!

YIKES!

IT COULD BE *ANYWHERE!*

I'M SURE WE'LL FIND HER.

WE NEED TO THINK LIKE A SNAKE.

"WE SEARCHED ALL DAY AND, STILL, NO SIGN OF CALLA...

WHAT A *NIGHTMARE!*

39

"I FEEL AWFUL. MARINA IS AFRAID TO EVEN GO TO SLEEP...

TELL ME THIS IS A *BAD DREAM*.

WE TURNED THIS HOUSE UPSIDE DOWN. WHERE COULD SHE BE?

I HAVE NO IDEA. LET'S GET SOME SLEEP. SHE'LL TURN UP.

THAT'S WHAT I'M *AFRAID* OF.

HUBBLE, WHAT WOULD YOU DO?

EAT HIM..

"WHEN MARINA FINALLY FALLS ASLEEP...

ZZZZ!

SNORE!

SSSS!

SSSS!

EEEEEEEEEEEK!

FOUND HER.

HEH HEH.

"ON SATURDAYS, A.J. AND HER DAD LIKE TO WORK TOGETHER ON HIS COOL CAR THAT WE PAINTED TO LOOK LIKE A LADY BUG...

A.J., HAND ME THAT SCREWDRIVER, PLEASE?

RING

HELLO?...IT IS? GREAT NEWS, WE'LL BE RIGHT OVER!

WHAT'S UP, DAD?

THAT WAS DR. CHO. BO'S WHEELS HAVE ARRIVED.

YES!

BO, IT'S TIME!

"A.J. AND HER FAMILY WASTED NO TIME IN TAKING BO FOR HIS NEW SET OF WHEELS...

IT'S SNUG, BUT IT FITS HIM. A.J., BE SURE THE HARNESS DOESN'T RUB IN SPOTS.

HE MAY NOT LIKE IT UNTIL HE GETS USED TO IT. TRY A TREAT TO SEE IF HE'LL WALK TO YOU.

HERE, BO! COME ON, BOY.

HE'S NOT MOVING!

PATIENCE, A.J.

WANT A YUMMY, YUMMY COOKIE?

THAT'S ONE STUBBORN DOG! LET'S TAKE HIM HOME TO PRACTICE!

41

"WE ALL CAME TO A.J.'S HOUSE TO MEET *BO* AND HELP A.J. ...

SEE, HE WON'T MOVE!

HMM...WHAT ANIMAL DOESN'T LIKE FOOD?

IF HE WON'T EAT HIS TREAT...

...I WILL!

NOW YOU'RE HUNGRY?!

WOO-HOO! WAY TO GO, HUBBLE!

42

CHAPTER SEVEN: PETS ON PARADE

"NOW THAT BO WAS ROLLING, SO WERE OUR SCHOOL'S EFFORTS TO HELP THE SHELTER. SUZY, OUR SUPER-FAVE WYXZ REPORTER AND EARHART FAN, WAS EXCITED TO TELL OUR STORY...

WE ARE LIVE AT EARHART'S PET PARADE TO BENEFIT THE McCLEAN COUNTY ANIMAL SHELTER THAT SUSTAINED TERRIBLE TORNADO DAMAGE. THERE'S STILL TIME TO DONATE PET FOOD AND TOYS...JUST DROP THEM OFF AT EARHART!

MY FOSTER PET, HANK, AND I ARE PARADE GRAND MARSHALS, AND WE'LL BE SPOTLIGHTING ALL THE FOSTER PETS IN THE PARADE TODAY.

≶WOOF≷

OUR FIRST FOSTER PET IS JOSIE THE MACAW AND HER FOSTER PARENT, ZARA KUMAR! ZARA TAUGHT JOSIE AND EARHART'S THIRD GRADERS SOME COOL MOVES...

♫ TO THE RIGHT... TO THE RIGHT... TO THE LEFT... TO THE LEFT... ♫

♫ "LET'S CUPID SHUFFLE!" ♫

♫ DOWN. DOWN. DO YOUR DANCE! DO YOUR DANCE! ≶CAW!≷ ♫

43

YEE-HAW! OUR NEXT ENTRY IS HEADED TO THE WILD WEST! GIDDY-YAP THERE, COWGIRL, AND LOOK AT BO'S *FANCY WHEELS!* GREAT JOB, A.J.!

FROM THE AMERICAN WEST, TO OUR OWN BACKYARDS WE HAVE TALENTED FOSTER PETS! LUCY MONROE FOUND A NICE BIG MOUSE FOR CALLA THE CORN SNAKE, WHICH IS A CONSTRICTER. THAT'S A BIG SQUEEZE!

AND LOOK AT EARHART'S *BAND STUDENTS* DRESSED TO SUPPORT OUR ANIMAL SHELTER! HANK, I WANT A POODLE ONESIE. WHAT DO YOU THINK?

OH, LOOK, IT'S SOFIA DRESSED AS *REY* IN A STAR BATTLE. SOFIA IS A TALENTED ARTIST. SHE CREATED THAT DEATHSTAR WITH HER GUINEA PIGS AS STAR FIGHTER PILOTS!

THAT'S HER MOM PULLING THE FLOAT. PEDAL POWER MAKES THE JETS GO AROUND!

AND, OUR FINAL FLOAT! THERE HE IS...HUBBLE AND HIS PRIDE OF SHELTER CATS. TRULY HE'S THE *KING!*

BOW! MY PEOPLE!

PRIDE OF EARHART

45

WOW! WHAT A WAY TO END THE PARADE! EARHART STUDENTS, PARENTS, AND TEACHERS HAVE COME TOGETHER...

LOOK AT ALL THE *DONATIONS!* NEW FOOD, TOYS, AND COZY BLANKETS. WHAT DO YOU SAY, HANK?

RUFF! RUFF!

DOG FOOD DOG FOOD

FISH FOOD FISH FOOD FISH FOOD

CAT FOOD CAT FOOD

"THE SHELTER'S *GRAND RE-OPENING* IS SO EXCITING. THE PET SHELTER IS BETTER THAN BEFORE. IT'S TIME TO MAKE SURE IT'S SUPER COZY WITH BEDS, BRAND NEW FOOD, TOYS...

A.J., THIS IS AMAZING! LET'S FIND DR. CHO AND SEE WHAT'S INSIDE!

"...AND THE COOLEST DONATIONS OF ALL...BIG SUPER-AWESOME RECYCLED COMFY CHAIRS! EARHART SECOND GRADERS HAVE PLEDGED TO PRACTICE READING AND GIVE THE PUPS SOME COMPANY AT THE SAME TIME.

"AND THE MAMA BEAR SAID...

THE DOGS ARE *LISTENING!* WILL BO GET A CHAIR?

YEP, AND I HAVE *GOOD NEWS* ABOUT BO THAT I'LL TELL YOU ABOUT AFTER OUR TOUR...

48

HERE'S THE *CAT ROOM.* THE DOGGIES HAVE FANCY CHAIRS WHILE THE CATS HAVE THEIR OWN NEW *PLAYGROUND* THAT'S PERFECT FOR CLIMBING AND SCRATCHING.

THIS IS THE COOLEST CAT ROOM EVER!

CATS *RULE. DOGS DROOL.*

49

AND HERE WE HAVE OUR *JUNGLE* ROOM FOR--

THIS ROOM IS THE *BOMB!*

RABBITS AND GUINEA PIGS WILL LOVE IT.

IT'S PERFECT FOR BIRDS.

CALLA AND HER SNAKE FRIENDS WILL LOVE HANGING ON THE BRANCHES.

YES, AND NOT HANGING OUT IN MY ROOM!

GOOD THINGS *CAN* HAPPEN, EVEN AFTER A BAD STORM! NOW I PROMISED NEWS FOR ALL OF YOU...LET'S GO TO MY OFFICE.

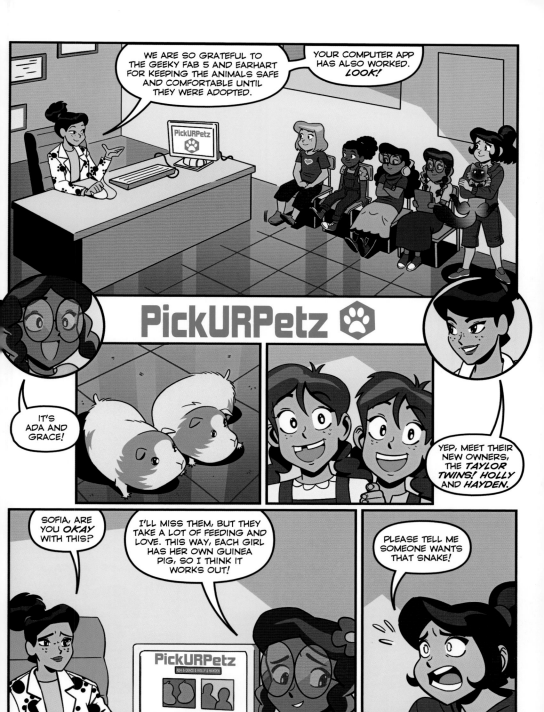

WE ARE SO GRATEFUL TO THE GEEKY FAB 5 AND EARHART FOR KEEPING THE ANIMALS SAFE AND COMFORTABLE UNTIL THEY WERE ADOPTED.

YOUR COMPUTER APP HAS ALSO WORKED. *LOOK!*

PickURPetz

PickURPetz 🐾

IT'S ADA AND GRACE!

YEP, MEET THEIR NEW OWNERS, THE *TAYLOR TWINS!* HOLLY AND *HAYDEN.*

SOFIA, ARE YOU *OKAY* WITH THIS?

I'LL MISS THEM, BUT THEY TAKE A LOT OF FEEDING AND LOVE. THIS WAY, EACH GIRL HAS HER OWN GUINEA PIG, SO I THINK IT WORKS OUT!

PickURPetz
ADA & GRACE & HOLLY & HAYDEN
MATCHED!

PLEASE TELL ME SOMEONE WANTS THAT SNAKE!

51

YEP, MEET *CARL!* HE'S A PHOTOGRAPHER WITH A BIG AQUARIUM FOR CALLA!

YES! NO MORE SNAKES IN MY BED!

HAS ANYONE ASKED FOR JOSIE?

AND BO?

YES, THEY BOTH HAVE BEEN CHOSEN... UNLESS YOU WANT TO KEEP THEM.

THIS IS SO HARD! BUT, MY FAMILY IS GONE ALL DAY. BO NEEDS HELP WITH HIS LEGS.

I KNOW, A.J. WE SHARED SO MUCH WITH JOSIE AND BO. BUT MY MOM SAYS IT ISN'T ALWAYS ABOUT ME, AND I HAVE TO THINK OF WHAT'S BEST FOR OTHERS, AND THAT MEANS PETS, TOO.

LET ME SHOW YOU WHO WANTS TO ADOPT THEM...

PickURPetz
WENDELL & BO
MATCHED!

PickURPetz 🐾

OHMYGOSH, HE LOOKS LIKE BO!

WENDELL'S A RETIRED FARMER WITH LOTS OF TIME TO HELP BO...AND HIS FARM HAS PLENTY OF SPACE TO RUN!

PickURPetz 🐾

AND THIS IS *JOANNA STILES!* SHE IS A SOPRANO AND MUSIC PROFESSOR AT THE UNIVERSITY.

SHE AND JOSIE CAN SING TOGETHER!

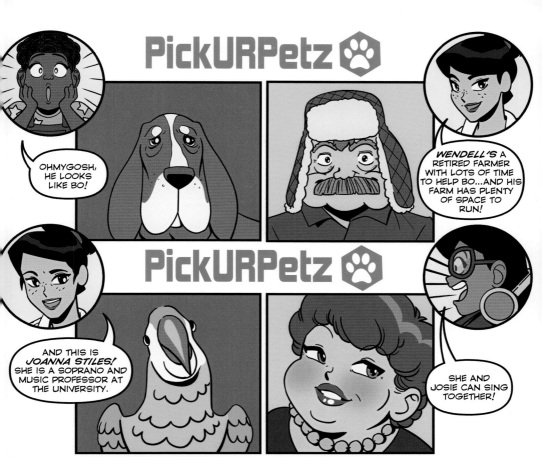

FEEL BETTER?

YES!

BUT WHAT ABOUT THE KITTIES AND HANK?

I ALWAYS SAID THAT TEACHING FOURTH GRADE CAN BE LIKE WRANGLING KITTIES...AND IT'S *TRUE!*

WELL, HEY THERE, GEEKY FAB 5!

YOU GIRLS DIDN'T THINK I COULD LIVE WITHOUT HANK, DID YOU?!

THANKS TO THE *GEEKY FAB 5,* I'VE GOT THE BESTEST NEW FRIEND!

I CAN'T WAIT TILL I GO TO *MARS*...THERE'S NO SNAKES THERE!

MCCLEAN COUNTY NO-KILL ANIMAL SHELTER

⸕HISS!⸕ I'M NOT SURE HOW I FEEL ABOUT SUZY AND THAT...*DOG!*

"AND SO OUR STORY ABOUT THE TORNADO DISASTER HAS A HAPPY ENDING. MISS MALONE DECIDED TO KEEP THE KITTIES AND HANK IS NOW SUZY'S BEST FRIEND. (HUBBLE WILL GET OVER IT.) EVERYONE HAS A FOREVER HOME, AND FOR THE SHELTER PETS, A PLACE TO LIVE SAFE AND HAPPY UNTIL THEY ARE ADOPTED. EVEN AFTER BAD STORMS THE SUN ALWAYS SHINES AGAIN!"

WATCH OUT FOR PAPERCUTZ

Welcome to the tougher-than-a-tornado third GEEKY F@B 5 graphic novel, "DOGgone CATastrophe," by writers Lucy Lareau & her mom, Liz Lareau, and Ryan Jampole, Suzannah Rowntree, & Scott Couto, artists, brought to you by Papercutz, the pet-loving people dedicated to publishing great graphic novels for all ages. I'm Jim Salicrup, the Editor-in-Chief and volunteer pet-poop picker-upper, with a special behind-the-scenes look at GEEKY F@B 5...

We're going to talk a little about how a graphic novel is created with a focus on the artists who drew the first half of "DOGgone CATastrophe." As if erstwhile Papercutz Associate Editor Suzannah Rowntree wasn't busy enough, after penciling and inking a story for THE LOUD HOUSE #6 "Loud and Proud," she was able to produce 25 pages of layouts for GEEKY F@B 5! Scott Couto, who recently inked HOTEL TRANSYLVANIA #2-3 plus a few stories for THE LOUD HOUSE, was able to embellish Suzannah's pages in the GEEKY F@B 5 style. For those of you wondering exactly what I'm talking about ("Penciling" "inking," "embellish," etc.), let me explain...

There are many ways to go about creating a graphic novel. Some are written, drawn, lettered, and colored all by one person. Raina Telgemeier, the brilliant creator of such graphic novels as "Smile," "Sisters," "Ghost," and others, is such a creator. Other graphic novels, like GEEKY F@B 5, are produced by a team.

GEEKY F@B 5 starts with a script by the mother and daughter writing duo, Liz and Lucy Lareau. A graphic novel script is similar to a movie or TV script, except with a lot less scenes. Five minutes in a movie or TV show can convey a whole lot of story, but in comics, that could take anywhere from five to a hundred pages to tell the same story, depending on how complicated that story may be. Look at it this way, in just one minute of a movie, there is 1,440 frames of film. On one page of a graphic novel there can be anywhere from 1 to 8 panels. That's a really BIG difference! A key part of graphic novel story-telling is to be as concise as possible, to convey as much as possible.

Once the script is completed and edited (by Managing Editor Jeff Whitman and me), it's sent on to the artists to illustrate. With "DOGgone CATastrophe," Suzannah Rowntree did very tight layouts in pencil, drawing the scenes described in the script. For example, Suzannah drew a beautiful first page, that the writers thought might better serve the story if the angle was adjusted. Here's what Suzannah originally drew for the first page (Technical note: Full page panels in graphic novels are usually called splash pages.)...

And here's what she drew for the revised first page...

As you can see, Suzannah drew the page with a pencil. With today's digital technology, sometimes pencil art is all that's needed, but the style for GEEKY F@B 5 has been established by Ryan Jampole using slick ink lines. And that's where Scott Couto came in. He drew in ink over Suzannah's pencils, and made little adjustments to the art so that it would look consistent with Ryan's style.

Once the page is inked, Wilson Ramos Jr. digitally adds the letters – all the words, word balloons, captions, and sound effects – and either Laurie E. Smith or Leonard Ito digitally adds the color. And to see how that came out, just flip back to page 5. We hope you like the results as much as we do.

As I said, there are many ways to create a graphic novel. For example, writer David Gallaher and artist Steve Ellis collaborate in their own unique way on THE ONLY LIVING GIRL, their new Papercutz graphic novel series, a follow-up to their acclaimed Sci-fi/Fantasy series THE ONLY LIVING BOY. Take a look at THE ONLY LIVING GIRL in special preview on the following pages.

The particular way the Lucy, Liz, Suzannah, Scott, and Ryan work allows people who are especially talented in certain areas to just focus on their specialty. The writers handle the writing, the artists handle the art, and it all comes together as a GEEKY F@B 5 graphic novel. Not everyone can be both a brilliant writer and a great artist. Just like the GEEKY F@B 5 themselves, it took 5 writers and artists to create something together. We hope you enjoyed this little behind-the-scenes peek at how a graphic novel is created.

And of course, we hope you enjoyed "DOGgone CATastrophe." One of the ways to tell if a story is successful or not is by how people react to the characters, and with the GEEKY F@B 5, the response has been overwhelmingly positive. Everyone seems to have fallen in love with Lucy, Marina, Sofia, A.J., Zara, and even Hubble! So, I'm thrilled to announce that the GEEKY F@B 5 will return in their fourth graphic novel, "Food Fight for Fiona," coming soon to your favorite bookseller or local library. Don't miss it!

Thanks,

STAY IN TOUCH!

EMAIL: salicrup@papercutz.com
WEB: papercutz.com
TWITTER: @papercutzgn
INSTAGRAM: @papercutzgn
FACEBOOK: PAPERCUTZGRAPHICNOVELS
FAN MAIL: Papercutz, 160 Broadway, Suite 700, East Wing, New York, NY 10038

Lucy Loves Animals!

Hi, everyone! I am so excited about "DOGgone CATastrophe" because it's all about ANIMALS! Ever since I was little, I have always loved all kinds of animals. I even wrote about white rhinos in third grade and wanted to save them. We don't have rhinos in my neighborhood, but my friends and I all have pets! Do you? I have 3 cats. One of my friends has an old dog and a puppy who is learning not to bite. Another friend has two cats and two dogs. My other friend has a puppy Husky and two cats.

They are all so stinkin' cute! I love them all (except for the puppy that bites). This book was fun to write with my mom because it's about pets finding homes.

Kids at one of the schools in my own town helped our local pet shelter by raising money for food and toys. They even went to the shelter to practice reading to the dogs and to play with them. Sometimes my brother goes to the animal shelter with his girlfriend just to pet the kitties.

The PickURPetz app in this book is so cool. We got the idea when one of the characters in Lucy's class talks about his grandpa using the dating app to find friends! So, we thought, "What the heck? Pets are people too!" The app the girls create makes it easy for people to find the pet that fits best in their home.

The girls use their skills to make an app which is hard to do, but as the GEEKY F@B 5 always say, "When Girls Stick Together, We Can Do Anything!"

Hope you enjoyed reading!

Lucy
Lucy Lareau

P.S. In this GEEKY F@B 5 graphic novel, Sofia has two cute guinea pigs Ada and Grace. It must have been fate! Do you know why? Well, Sofia is a total computer geekette, and she recognized the furry little guineas names as the same as two famous women pioneers in computing. Coincidence? Possibly, but we prefer to think the app factored their names into the equation when deciding Sofia would be the perfect match for Ada and Grace. Who were the original Ada and Grace? Ada Lovelace, was actual English royalty! She was a mathematician who laid the foundation for computer coding. Ada lived in the 1800s. The other amazing computer scientist, Grace Hopper, was a rear admiral in the US Navy. She managed the huge early computers and even came up with the term "computer bug" when she found a moth in an early computer! She died in 1992. Both women are amazing and paved the way for women to be successful in technology!

I REMEMBER THE FIRST DAY I SAW MY FATHER SMILE.

HOW DOES IT FEEL TO HAVE YOUR DAUGHTER FOLLOW IN YOUR FOOTSTEPS, DOCTOR PARFITT?

I COULDN'T BE PROUDER.

AS THE ONLY CHILD OF THE AWARD-WINNING ASTROPHYSICIST, CELEBRATED AUTHOR, AND RENOWNED EDUCATOR...

I ONLY WISH HER MOTHER WAS HERE TO SEE THIS.

I ALWAYS FELT HE BLAMED ME FOR HER LOSS.

AND IT HAUNTED ME...

SO... YOU'RE ERIK, RIGHT?

UMMM... YES?

...EVERYWHERE I WENT.

I WAS ONLY SIX WEEKS OLD WHEN SHE DIED.

I NEVER GOT TO KNOW HER.

I'M ZANDRA.

YEAH. FROM DR. GLASSER'S CLASS.

I WAS WONDERING IF YOU'VE THOUGHT ABOUT A LAB PARTNER FOR NEXT SEMESTER?

AND SHE NEVER GOT TO KNOW ME.

SHE NEVER GOT TO LEARN ABOUT THE GIRL I HAD BECOME.

IN HER ABSENCE, I TRIED SO HARD TO BE DADDY'S LITTLE GIRL.

AFTER I WON THE SCHOLARSHIP, I DID WHAT I COULD TO WIN HIS APPROVAL.

METS

So the aim of quantum gravity is only to describe the quantum behavior of the gravitational field... interesting.

I WAS A GOOD STUDENT...

UHHHHHH... UH...NO. YOU?

YES, THAT'S WHY I'M TALKING TO YOU, SILLY.

FOR OUR PROJECT, I WAS HOPING TO TEST THE QUANTUM MECHANICS OF GRAVITY.

RIGHT.

OH.

BUT FOCUSING ON NON-GRAVITATIONAL FORCES?

...ONE OF THE BEST.

IT NEVER FELT LIKE IT WAS ENOUGH.

NOT NOW, ZEE. I'M TRYING TO SOLVE THIS EQUATION.

BUT I KEPT TRYING.

I LEARNED EVERYTHING I COULD FROM MY FATHER.

I KNOW QUITE A BIT ABOUT GRAVITY AND YOU SEEM TO KNOW A COUPLE OF THINGS ABOUT SCIENCE AND STUFF.

"MAKE EVERY DAY JEALOUS OF YESTERDAY" WAS HIS MOTTO.

ON THOSE BLEAK NIGHTS WHEN MY FATHER WOULD WORK LATE...

...I BROUGHT MY IDEAS TO LIFE.

MY ONLY LIMITS...

DONT WALK

...WERE THE DARK RECESSES OF MY IMAGINATION.

SURE, I MADE MISTAKES.

COME ON, JUPITER, YOU KNOW YOUR ORBIT ISN'T THAT LOW.

BUT THEY WERE MY MISTAKES TO MAKE.

DONT WALK

AND I MADE A LOT OF THEM.

BUT I ALWAYS TRIED TO LEARN FROM THEM.

SOME MISTAKES STICK WITH YOU.

THESE LIGHTS, HUH?

YEAH. THEY TAKE FOREVER.

SOME MISTAKES HAUNT YOU.

62

REGARDLESS, I ALWAYS TRIED TO DO MY BEST.

HOPING IT WOULD BE GOOD ENOUGH.

AND THEN THEY CHANGE SO QUICK.

YOU ALMOST HAVE TO RUN TO OUTRACE THEM.

SOMETIMES YOUR BEST ISN'T GOOD ENOUGH...

BUT THEN AGAIN... SOMETIMES IT IS...

AMAZING!

YOU CAN'T JUST WAIT FOR SUCCESS TO HAPPEN.

OR LIFE WILL PASS YOU BY.

WITH *THIS* ONE AS LEVERAGE, HE WILL BE COMPELLED TO TELL US HIS SECRETS.

A MODEL OF THE SOLAR SYSTEM IS BENEATH YOUR TALENTS, ZEE.

BUT IT ISN'T GUARANTEED EITHER.

Harris County Public Library
Houston, Texas

WANNA RACE?

YOU BET.

MY FAILURES MADE ME MORE COMPETITIVE.

I DID EVERYTHING I COULD TO MAKE MY FATHER NOTICE ME...

...TO SHOW HIM THAT HE COULD BE PROUD OF ME AGAIN.

RUN!

BUT IN THE END, IT DIDN'T MATTER.

BECAUSE I LEARNED SOMETHING VERY IMPORTANT ABOUT LOVE THAT DAY.

5

Continued in THE ONLY LIVING GIRL #1
"The Island at the Edge of Infinity" available at booksellers everywhere.